MASKS IN

JEAN LORRAIN (1855-1906) was the pseudonym of Paul Alexandre Martin Duval. He was one of the leading figures of the Decadent Movement and the author of numerous novels, volumes of poetry and short stories. At one point he was probably the highest paid journalist in France. Though mostly remembered today for his famous duel with Marcel Proust, he might be seen as the true chronicler of the *fin-de-siècle*. His short story collections *Nightmares of an Ether-Drinker* and *The Soul-Drinker and Other Decadent Fantasies* were previously published by Snuggly Books.

BRIAN STABLEFORD has been publishing fiction and non-fiction for fifty years. His fiction includes a series of "tales of the biotech revolution" and a series of metaphysical fantasies featuring Edgar Poe's Auguste Dupin. He is presently researching a history of French *roman scientifique* from 1700-1939 for Black Coat Press, translating much of the relevant material into English for the first time, and also translates material from the Decadent and Symbolist Movements. He has previously translated for Snuggly Books a number of titles, including *The Unknown Collaborator and Other Legendary Tales* by Victor Joly and *Bluebirds* by Catulle Mendès.

SNUGGLY BOOKS

JEAN LORRAIN

MASKS IN THE TAPESTRY

Translated by

BRIAN STABLEFORD

THIS IS A SNUGGLY BOOK

ISBN: 978-1-943813-37-7

CONTENTS

MASKS IN THE TAPESTRY

FUTILE VIRTUE

D URING the three long days that he had been riding through the dunes florid with pale thistles, no sail had whitened the horizon. There was, from dawn to dusk, the monotonous immensity of a calm sea, a sea without a wrinkle, the color of slate, beneath the dismal pallor of a white sky.

Sometimes, his horse stopped abruptly, hooves forward, and whinnied toward the sea, and in a silky flutter of wings, gulls disturbed from some hole in the cliff would circle high in the air, and the russet sand would be dappled by their shadows. The young man did not even raise his head. His face grave beneath the spread wings of the eagle on his helmet, he walked pensively to the foot of the cliff. It was a high wall of schist running for leagues on end alongside the sad sea. Desiccated grass, almost mauve, hanging down from the flank of the rock like hanks of dead hair, and a few rare sea-birds, were its only inhabitants.

In the evening, the cliffs became pink, and even the dunes caught fire in the blaze of the sunset. The young man, dismounting, allowed his horse to graze on the blue thistles of the sands, and tried to slake his own thirst, and his hunger too, by chewing the salty flesh of some shellfish. Then, beneath the rising moon, he continued on his way.

In the cloister where he had been brought up on the orders of his mother, the Queen, he had made a vow to find, dead or alive, the knight with the fair hair to whom he owed his life. Bertram was the fruit of a sin.

An adulterous bastard of the Queen of Aquitaine, he had been brooded and nourished like the very idea of vengeance; the adulterous process had sworn to find, by way of the son of her lust, the unfaithful lover who had abandoned her. A Barnabite convent had seen the young Prince grow up; the Queen had presided over his education, invisible and masked, unknown to the son she destined for a tragic denouement. The monks had raised the child harshly, in the hatred of amour, women and everything that laughs and flourishes under heaven; fasting and prayer had made a rude soul of the Queen's son. Bertram wore a cilice beneath his damascened armor and a triple cord of hemp around his waist.

Then, one morning, intoxicated by a philter, the palms of his hands and the soles of his feet rubbed with the blood of a she-wolf, the young avenger had been released into the world.

"You will recognize the man who has made your childhood obscure and mortified by the triple emerald that shines in the crest of his helmet, where it is embedded. Whether his hair be golden or white, strike and kill, and you will have avenged your humiliated life, your mother, your race and your God."

Those fateful words had been pronounced by a voice of dream in the chapel of the convent where Bertram had awaited the call to arms. A form hidden in the shadows had dictated the decree. The next day, at dawn, Bertram had ridden away, gauntleted, armored, masked from the annealed silver of his helmet-crest to the stars of his spurs, with, above his motion, the double gleam of raw gold of an enormous eagle beating its wings.

High in the convent's bell-tower, a woman had followed him for a long time with her eyes into the ruddy light of the nascent day. When the silhouette of the young adventurer had disappeared into the heath, the Queen had gone to prostrate herself before the main altar, and night had surprised her there, muttering and praying.

Now that he was riding in the moonlight, which silvered the calm sea, the memory of strange encounters oppressed the young warrior.

Firstly, on the third evening after his departure from the convent, there had been the apparition of three young women on the edge of a wood, the three daughters of the old lord, as they had named themselves when saluting him in a familiar fashion, addressing him by name. Sitting at the entrance to the forest, they had risen to their feet on seeing him and had tried to garland the bridle of his palfrey with flowers. They were enticing and joyful, with chaplets of anemones in their mobile tresses, and seemed to be naked beneath their new tunics of flower-patterned silk. Standing in the dew, they had enveloped him with their group as in a playful round-dance, and with their attitude, the caress of their gazes, their voices, and their supple and youthful arms, they had attempted to retain him—but he had driven his horse forward rudely, at the risk of knocking them over; the elves of the meadows had the custom of appearing to travelers thus in the evenings, and he had spurred his mount on under the branches, grimly and willfully deaf to their appeals.

He had ridden for two nights and two days through the forest of oaks, and then the high shade had given way to vast clearings, and the clearings to bleak plains traversed by curtains of aspens; pools were mirrored there amid the long grass, where vapors floated night and day, weaving around the equivocal trunks of willows the appearances of shrouds. Then he had entered a region of peat-bogs and marshes, where the black soil yielded underfoot. And, on one moonless night, when he was going along the edge of one of those lugubrious marshes, his palfrey had suddenly reared up beneath him, and Bertram, having looked up, had perceived a supernatural and livid beauty standing on the leaden water.

It was the body of a woman, frightful in her pallor, but her eyes and her smile were steeped in a strange ecstasy. She had surged forth like a fire follet above a clump of nenuphars, and smiled wryly, as if writhing in a spasm, her back arched and her mouth open, with a little silver mirror in her hand.

An unexpected moon had sprung forth at the same time behind the osier-beds, and, as everything was nacred by its reflections, the blissful dead woman had barred the young man's passage, simultaneously extending toward him her blue-tinted lips and the silver of the mirror. An old defoliated willow had suddenly reflected in the pool the silhouette of a faun, and the young warrior, having rejected with horror the immodest cadaver, an enormous frog had abruptly hopped between the tufts of grass and plunged into the pallid water with a dull plop.

Bertram, while marching along the strand, thought about those sortileges, all those tricks and all those illusions.

What did those masques of shadow, those figures wandering by night want with him, and what was the symbolism of all those temptations?

He saw then that a silent galley, of which he had perceived neither the friction of sails not the plash of oars, was going along the shore in parallel with him; the tall masts, the rigging and the sheets stood out transparently in the darkness, and one might have thought it a ship of dream, for it was gliding over the water rather than cleaving the waves, and everyone aboard seemed to be asleep; no sailor was on deck. An abandoned vessel or a phantom ship? The waves were not even splashing around its flanks, and it advanced mysteriously, the color of ash, alongside him.

Bertram would have believed himself the victim of another vision if he had not distinguished, leaning on his elbows at the prow, a motionless old man, doubtless the pilot, whose fingers were tormenting a lyre—but an enchanted lyre, for the touched strings did not produce any sound.

When the daylight appeared, Bertram found himself in a region of valleys and small hills, divided by vivid hedges and apple-orchards. The phantom vessel, the strand of pink sand and the high cliff had vanished, and the young adventurer, who was beginning not to be astonished by anything any longer, spurred his mount between the meadows and the hawthorn hedges of the land or orchards. There was, in any case, the most profound solitude. One sensed that the sea was not far away by the hue of the sky, swept by clouds, and the apple-trees twisted by the wind.

He had been riding for five long hours along a kind of sunken road when a beautiful lady appeared to him.

She was entirely clad in a brocade patterned with aspen leaves, as slender and upright as a lily, mounted bareback on a unicorn, an elegant and fabulous beast of dream, whose coat was as shiny as metal.

The lady on the unicorn wore a golden helmet over her black hair surmounted by a little crown, and was holding a couched lance, like a knight.

She barred the young sire's path, but while she threatened with her lance she belied her evil intention with a smile, and indicated to Bertram with her finger a bleeding rose in her girdle. But he had nothing in his head but the idea of murder; he brushed the beautiful warrior's steel-tipped lance aside with his sword, and passed on.

The beautiful lady whipped his face as he passed with the rose from her girdle, but it was only a desiccated rose that brushed the young man, and having turned round in surprise, he only saw an old woman fleeing at a gallop on a donkey.

Another ambush set by the Evil One, he thought, and went on his way, slightly sad and slightly weary.

He finally arrived at an inn of sorts. A pin-branch shaded the door, and three beautiful young women were standing in front of the threshold. Their breasts free in russet jackets, bare-headed and barefoot, they were cheerful and robust in the warm dusk. One was spinning with a distaff, another, leaning over a stone trough, was reeling up the thread; as for the third, at the sight of the young man she ran precipitately into the inn, only to come out again with a pitcher of wine. She offered Bertram a drink, and the other two urged him to dismount. They smelled of sweat, bread and lavender, but Bertram pushed them away. They went back inside then, with loud bursts of laughter, closing the door of the inn, and Bertram remained alone in the road.

The horse had approached the trough in order to drink from it, and as the palfrey did so, Bertram, who had leaned forward, uttered a cry.

The royal adventurer had just seen his own image appear in the depths of the trough, which had reflected it, and it was the face of an old man with a long white beard that was looking back at him, with a sad and weary gaze and a forgiving smile: a pale face of yore, circled by a golden helmet on which there were three emerald tears—and Bertram recognized the man he had to strike.

It was himself, therefore, that he had to kill by striking his image, and, his heart gripped by an infinite sadness, Bertram understood that he had grown old. That white hair and those dull eyes before his own eyes were his, alas, and he understood, too late, that he had embarked on an impossible adventure. It had been necessary for him to live his life without disdaining love, sensuality, pleasure and even fleeting opportunity, but he had been lured by a deceptive mirage, like the pilot of the silent vessel.

But it was necessary not to think of turning back, for every hour flees, irreparably. . . .

17

THE PRINCE IN THE FOREST

I
THE GUARDIAN

IS it a tale read yesterday or a dream of my childhood whose décor and characters are haunting me?
Either way, it is an obsession that extends as far as
malaise, and without being able to specify in what book
of legends or collection of fairy tales I saw the mysterious and hallucinatory image, the memory solicits me
everywhere, and brings me back to an obscure and very
high forest, as high as a cathedral, with its groves of
birches as polished as pillars, and clumps of fir trees here
and there bathed in blue-tinted gleams, and undergrowth
illuminated, even in broad daylight, as if by somnolent
moonlight.

A strange forest, in truth: footfalls make no sound
there; the azure filters through the high branches on to
the ground strewn with pine-needles, devoid of a single
sprig of moss or any flower. Sometimes, a chimerical
blue calyx was glimpsed between two trees, some iris of
dream blooming there in the veritably disturbing calm
of that wood—but at closer range, it was just a patch
of light descended from the vault, or some fragment of
rough bark splashed by the sun; for everything becomes

blue in that forest of dream and silence, a silence whose absent sonority causes anguish.

How does the Prince who has been wandering there for hours come to be there? Does he even know himself? Yes, now he remembers the pursuit of a whistling jay hopping from branch to branch and tree to tree, at the extremity of his park. Charmed by the bird's chirping, the seduction of a dream—to which he was not inclined, however—he had gone through the gate and had almost immediately found himself in the silent, blue-tinted forest, which he had never seen before, although he knew the country for twenty leagues around, being a great rider and hunter of wild beasts.

The whistling Jay itself had disappeared. There were no birds in the forest; it was profoundly calm and somber, and that great silence had reassured the Prince at first, the property of enchanted places being the appearance of bare feet on the moss and the sound of bursts of laughter, distant music and insidious youthful voices. There was none of that at the feet of those giant birches, spaced out like the columns of a temple—but at length that symmetry alarmed him and the great calm ended up gripping him by the heart. Then again, the solitude of those trees was completely unfamiliar to him.

Like an immense madrepore it had suddenly surged forth in front of him; that was suggestive of sortilege and nightmare, and the forest must have been very large, extending for league after league through the region, for he had been walking for hours, oppressed by the frightening calm of the woods devoid of birds, with motionless foliage, in which the life of the saps seemed to have been congealed, where not a single breath of wind soughed in the treetops, where no woodcutter appeared in the distance among severed stumps, for the forest was deserted, and the distress of that abandonment was such that he would have preferred the danger of no matter what encounter to that strange solitude.

As an increasing terror began to bathe his temples with sweat, a face suddenly appeared before him: an anguished face, ardent and sorrowful, the eyes infinitely heartsick, aflame and empty, with all the features wasted and the corners of the lips taut: an indescribable expression of suffering and pity.

An enormous crown of thorns—the same crown with which religious painters circle the head of the Savior—radiated behind it, gigantically; and in the livid nimbus of the face, hollowed out by tears, a kind of host was framed, with the pallor of death, but of blissful death, for some unknown ecstasy transfigured the face of the dolorous apparition entirely.

She was standing erect against the ultramarine backcloth of a clump of firs, with one hand pressing to her dress, over her heart, a bouquet of livid blue dune-thistles, whose glaucous foliage was stained with blood; and all of her tortured face was resplendent in the crown of thorns, like a blue flame, the same blue as her eyes, of an intoxicating azure.

The Prince stopped, dazzled and terrified but nevertheless charmed.

Then in a grave and profound voice, she said: "You don't recognize me, being too young as yet to have encountered me before. Those who have known me, alas make no mistake, and I have no need to appear before them in all the pomp of my sad splendor to see them fall immediately to their knees and implore me, the poor people, with infantile cries and womanly sobs. I am the guardian of this forest; I alone can enable you to get out of it, and lead you back to life, to the world, to everything that is not deception and mirage. I have lived longer than ten thousand years, and yet I shall never grow old; the blood of my wounds will be forever fresh. My name is Dolor.

Instinctively, the Prince had knelt down, his gaze drinking in the unexpected young woman, whose feet did not seem to be touching the ground.

Then, placing on the Prince's forehead a frail but astonishingly heavy hand, she said: "And you don't even know the name of the forest into which the whistling jay has led you, for you have not come here either on the heels of Amour or those of Youth. It's by virtue of distraction that you yielded to the spell, and it's for that reason that I can save you. You're in the forest of Dream. These high woods of slumber and silence, whose august tranquility frightens you, you might perhaps regret all your life; their deceptive memory will haunt you until your dying day, but be thankful nevertheless for having encountered me, because in one hour more, you might have gone to sleep here forever.

"How many I have woken up, in my anxious wanderings, who would otherwise have been engulfed in eternal slumber! And how many I have come across too late! And then, I confess, how many I have allowed to go to sleep, for pity's sake. So much did the reflection of

24

dream transfigure their poor faces, that for them, seeing them so happy in the inanity of their dreams, I hesitated, and went on my way without applying my finger to their closed eyelids, fearing for them the cruelties of the future."

And Dolor, with a voice steeped in tenderness, added: "But your weary eyes are already closing, poor child. Respond, make an effort: are you ready to follow me? I can still save you, but I cannot restore you to reality without frightful anguish. Are you prepared to suffer?"

The Prince, this time mute with fear, bowed his head without uttering a word.

"I am not a vain apparition come to draw tears from you; I am the very reality of life; my name is Dolor, and I have not lied in order to frighten you, poor being. This forest of mystery is more populous than you think. Look."

And, the blue-tinted figure having made a broad gesture with her extended hand, the depths of the forest suddenly became resplendent with a bleak pallor, and mingled with the ivory of bones and skulls, bodies appeared in the gaps, which might as easily have been sleeping humans as immobile cadavers, and the forest of Dream became, momentarily, a crypt of death.

With a bound the Prince came to his feet. "Take me away, take me away; I'll follow you, sympathetic phantom. I can no longer bear the sinister visions that surge forth at your voice."

With an immense pity in her tearful eyes, Dolor said: "And you won't complain about the bloodied feet, the palms pierced by nails, the flesh hollowed out by wounds?"

The Prince shook his head negatively.

"Come."

And Dolor, taking the young man by the wrist, drew him through the light-dappled gloom of the birches and the pines; but he was already no longer listening to her. He had stopped, his gaze ecstatic, in order to contemplate the luminous forms of women that had just appeared in the treetops. As if caught by their great wings in the branches and the foliage, like hanging virgins, they populated the high vaults of the forest, and their floating dresses were like snowy streaks of frost amid the verdure.

"Dreams," whispered Dolor, mysteriously, and placing a finger over his lips, she added: "Don't wake them."

But already, a melodious flutter of wings was running through the high branches, and, his bewildered eyes now fixed on the vertiginous forms, without even noticing that the majority among them resembled the dead, with their closed eyelids and waxen faces, as if gathered beneath the folds of their shadowy wings, without seeing, finally, that some were grimacing and green, hiding the faces of hags beneath membranous bat-wings, the Prince suddenly sank into some unspecifiable marvelous ecstasy, released his wrist from Dolor's grip, let himself slide to the ground at her feet, and in a voice that was already drowsy, said: "Go away; I'm afraid of your bloodstained dress, afraid of your eyes of folly, burned by tears; go away, I want to go to sleep."

And Dolor, resigned once again, resumed her wandering through the forest of which she is the guardian.

II
HIC FELICITAS

The reasonable will have lasted,
The unreasonable will have lived.
Chamfort.

THE PRINCE woke up. How long had his dream lasted? An hour? A century? With a surprised gaze, he scanned his surroundings, which he no longer recognized. The high, profound forest of firs and birches with the felted ground bathed in blue-tinted shadows, and its terrifying silent underwood, had disappeared. He had gone to sleep in the glaucous darkness of a forest of Dodona, but he found himself now on the side of a hill, sitting in short cut grass, sloping away gently toward an immense valley. Wooded hillocks, rather than hills, closed the horizon, and over all that nature, already touched by the rust of autumn, hung an insipid warm odor of damp leaves and ripe fruits, of a tender and sad sensuality, like a savor of bruised flesh, faded flowers and acorns: the odor of October, and perhaps of the tomb.

A pale blue sky, tufted with big white clouds with nacreous edges, weighed upon the hills like a lid. Three little ponds, irregular in form, were fuming in the hollow of the valley; violet vapors, like scarves, were floating gently over the reeds at the edges, and under the moist white sky the three sleeping lakes, like three great opals, shone with the bleak sheen of slow waters.

The landscape exhaled a great calm and a soft quietude, but vague rumors suddenly became audible, causing the Prince to prick up his ears and shake off his torpor. It was like the increasing, monotonous and lugubrious sound of cawing crows, and the Prince, having partly raised himself up from his bed of dry leaves, realized that the muffled clamors were coming from a forest of beeches already despoiled by the autumn; its reddened foliage blocked an entire corner of the valley, and the high crowns of unhealthy gold stood out from the hillsides, black with crows.

Their cawing now resounded through the countryside, incessant, angry and raucous: sometimes, a great cry of distress, emerging in the midst of the din, tore through it; and a great flock of black birds rose up from a point in the forest, taking flight briefly in order to settle further away; then, their chatter and sempiternal quarreling resumed, even more noisily. And from one end of the valley to the other, there was something akin to an enormous ear-splitting cackle of witches, whose monotony eventually gave rise to anguish.

The Prince felt ill. The calm of the décor was only apparent; he was well aware of that now. A malarial charm rose from those lakes; the mild atmosphere of the warm day, the soft white sky and the valley in pain were poisoned. There was a reek of corruption germinating in the odor of leaves and hay, floating miasmas nauseated him, and the increasing noise of battle, the forest populated by croaking beasts, troubled him. To what sinister work did those turbulent hordes of crows devote themselves?

The odor of the landscape's corruption now seemed to him to be coming from the forest. What, after all, were those cries of distress bursting out from time to time over the silence of the lakes, so swiftly stifled, as if by thrusts of claws and beaks? Innumerable black wings darkened the woods and sky with mourning; and, filled with a secret horror, the Prince wondered covertly what agonies and what scenes of carnage might be concealed by the yellow foliage of the strange forest with the reek of carrion.

As he leaned forward, trying—but in vain—to search that noisy corner of the valley with his gaze, the form of a woman, tall and slender, appeared some way below him. She was climbing the slope, walking with a light step; her feet, a trifle long, shod in violet silk, scarcely supported their toes on the dry grass. She had the rapid and lithe gait, with elevated heels, that Greek poets lent to goddesses, and everything, in fact, seemed immortal in that harmonious and delicate woman with her firm breasts, hard hips and closed white arms.

A dress of soft fabric floated around her body, a pale ash-gray in color, molded at the waist, and now that she was very close, the Prince admired the silver roses embroidered on the dress, with a neckline of pearls and kind of breastplate of gems over her bosom. It was a bizarrely wrought circlet made of gold plate studded with opals and pale pink, almost faded, topazes, which, dotted here and there with large pearls, gave her stature a kind of lunar splendor, a limpid and cold scintillation.

The same milky stones were heaped up in necklaces all the way to her ears, and sheathed her shoulders and arms with reflections.

But for her blonde hair, crowned with anemones and pearls floating into a sheet around her, one might have thought her a warrior princess, but the indolent insouciance of her physiognomy belied the costume, in spite of the profile of arrogant purity and beautiful sinuous lips. A vague smile attenuated her disdain.

In spite of the dazzling freshness of her cheeks and mouth, it was an effaced face, as if withdrawn from reality, appearing in a mist, and her eyes, indefinite in hue, devoid of depths and warmth, had the dull gleam of a sage jewel.

She was sumptuous, elegant, and charmless.

She came toward the Prince rapidly and, almost brushing him with her dress, snapped at him with a half-smile: "Where have you come from? What are you doing here? Come with me."

The Prince, half-raised up on his knees, gazed at her with surprised eyes.

"Let's go!" she added, touching his shoulder lightly. "Hurry up—I don't have time to waste. Believe me, follow my advice—don't allow yourself to be taken by surprise by the nocturnal vapors of this deadly valley. As soon as the sun sets, these woods and ponds emit a deadly chill. But I can't stop any longer. I'm expected up there, at the Castle of Wellbeing."

"The Castle of Wellbeing!" the young man exclaimed.

"And I can take you there; I alone know the way. I'm the reliable cure for past sufferings, evils still present and future alarms. I close the wounds of memory. My kiss scars and my touch hardens and firms up wretched bodies, as it tempers the soul against the possible blows of destiny; I deflect and defy the future. Get up and walk beside me, if some concern still remains to you for your salvation, and if you're not one of those cowards exhausted by illusions, in love with oblivion and desirous of dying."

The Prince, impressed by her curt speech, finally got to his feet and fell into step with her, curious about the stranger so certain of Wellbeing.

"The world has lived on my robust breath for ten thousand years," she said. "Greece adored me; its cities and its ports honored me in its temples until Asia Minor and Rome itself raised altars to me. I've had at my feet consuls, tribunes, famous debauchees and emperors laureate with gold; I've had poets crowned with violets, and even philosophers; sages have proclaimed me their daughter and although banished temporarily by Christ, my power is eternal. Since then I've expelled him in my turn from the sanctuary of hearts; I am health and life; my name is Indifference."

The Prince contemplated her with avid eyes. "And you know the road to Wellbeing? You know where it resides, and hides from our wretched eyes?"

"Yes," replied the stranger with the opal circlet, "I know the palace of repose and calm. You can already see its terraces protruding behind those tall cypresses in front of us and to one side."

The Prince trembled. "What! That peristyle with marble columns and those bronze busts in metal-lined niches, that Italian villa at the top of the hill, all white in its garden of pines and cypresses, is the haven desired by every creature, the Castle of Wellbeing?"

"Or that of Forgetfulness. Look."

They were standing under a white peristyle, in front of a motionless array of busts, and in those tall green-tinted faces the Prince discovered the features of known philosophers; the names of Zeno, Plato, Epictetus and Pythagoras came to his lips; but blind eyes of mat silver, like the gaze of specters, slept beneath their eyelids, and the Prince was afraid.

Around him was a symmetrical garden with narrow paths bordered with box-hedges. There was the rigid, seemingly varnished foliage of Spanish orange trees and Turbian laurels, and the obscure cones of pines and cypresses. A rectangular courtyard tiled with white and black marble opened, with a lively fountain at its exact center, whose jet sprang high in the air and fell back in a sheet into a jasper bowl ornamented at the corners with masks of green bronze.

In the garden, a pallid, plump young man was asleep, his body inert, his elbow leaning on the edge of the bowl and his hindquarters supported by a bench in a hemicycle dominated by a tall stele on which two words were written: *Hic felicitas.*[1] The water overflowing the cracked bowl was running over the black and white checkerboard and a glacial humidity, a moist freshness, imposed

---

1 *Felicitas*, Latin for good fortune, was sometimes deified in Rome. A famous inscription was found on the wall of a bakery in Pompeii, in which the legend *Hic habitat felicitas* (Good fortune resides here) was used as a caption for the very explicit depiction of a phallus.

a cellar-like atmosphere on the marble and the obscure garden. But the young man's sleep was so profound that he did not feel the water running over his feet and penetrating the soles of his white felt brodequins. His bloodless slender hands were holding a large book with an enamel clasp open on his knees. Desiccated poppies of a nacreous transparency were escaping from between the pages. Golden blond hair, of a singular suppleness, streamed like a liquid over his plump shoulders, and on that ponderous forehead, almost at the level of the wan eyelids, an invisible hand had placed a crown of enormous nenuphars.

Indifference then said: "*Hic felicitas.* Do you want to resemble him? You'll sleep like him. One is happy in the world when one forgets the world. Here, there's disdain for kisses and tears, dolors and joys. That murmurous water, ever renewed, even drowns memory. We have here the secret of wellbeing. Life cheats us; let is cheat life. Here is the safe refuge where one can be at ease, sit down, pause and sleep."

But the Prince felt a stupor invading his entire being; horror chilled him. That young man, asleep, as if buried alive in the green-tinted light and the coolness of the tomb in that shiny garden, the cadaverous inertia of the puffy flesh, rotting there in the running water, frightened him. Beneath his crown of nenuphars one might have thought him a drowned man, and the Prince thought within himself about the autumnal valley and the mystery of the three pools.

He did not articulate a single word, but his companion had understood. She shrugged her shoulders lightly.

"So be it. Return, then, to the crows, to the charnel-house of the forest, where the birds of prey pick vain Illusions—your sisters and your mistresses—to pieces with their beaks. Return to the edge of the lakes with the poisonous miasmas in which dreams are sketched, but don't complain if the crows of the valley peck out your eyes from their bloody orbits; you'll have wanted it. Go, then, suffer, bleed, return to Dolor, to Deception, to Life. Weep your tears until you shed the last drops of your heart's blood. But when, with your flesh rent by the claws of beasts, your feet bruised, and full of ulcers, you're stumbling, blind and desolate, through the forest of Murder, under the justiciary flight of the crows, at the feet of your tortured sisters, your dear Illusions, finally crucified to the trunks of the beeches by vengeful Destiny, don't hope to forget and to come back here to find calm. Go away—it's already too late."

Silent and pensive, the Prince was already descending toward the valley. He had resumed the road to the ponds.

THE TALE OF THE REAPERS

THERE was a great white wall in a path florid with thistles. The bare white wall, devoid of ivy, ran for leagues through the countryside; gnats were vibrating in the warm air, and a heavy August sun was causing the life of insects and grass to whisper.

Raymondin had been going along that wall of quarry-stone and plaster for hours. It had loomed up in front of him as he emerged from the town, at the top of the hill covered in sainfoin and lucerne. On the plateau haunted by blue butterflies—one might have thought them airborne campanulas—he had paused in order to look down, beneath his feet, at the town with its roofs, its ramparts, its bell-towers and the silvery ribbon of its river, in the black orbs of old bridges, and he had leaned on the old wall in order to relive a little of the life that he was leaving down there in the valley.

That was twenty years of his childhood, twenty years that he had slept through, as if drunk, in the bright gaiety of a golden summer, and the friendly town appeared to him with its streets, its crossroads, its nights of pale reveries, its calm and monotonous days, its cathedral with the portal that one might have thought made of gray cloth and the road to its calvary climbing between florid hedges; and Raymondin felt very emotional remembering, in some meadow, on the edge of some flowery wood, before or after the harvest, some primrose or favorite scabious, and he had wept in broad daylight today, as in all the days of the past, standing against the great white wall, and, without seeing a gray lizard asleep on a stone within the reach of his hand, he had wiped his tears away with the back of his sleeve, saying proudly: "This moment is mine, and I shall take it with me."

And he had set forth to follow the white wall, beneath the heavy August sun, and suddenly, by a path so grassy that he had not heard him coming, Raymondin had seen an old man, tall and straight, who had surged forth there, in the solitude, like a heat-induced vision. He was standing up, bare-headed, and seemed familiar; there was a kind of sadness of farewell in his smile, and, deaf and mute—for he did not speak—he showed Raymondin the horizon with a broad gesture, made with an iron key that he had in his hand.

And for the first time, Raymondin had experienced a frisson. A fear had taken hold of him that the white wall might only be that of a cemetery; but no crown of cypress or willow surpassed its summit.

He was immediately reassured and was about to go on when the tall old man had stopped him with a familiar gesture, and Raymondin had seen that they were both at the foot of a small tower: a small tower encased in the wall, and which scarcely surpassed it with the height of its tiled roof; a small round tower whose crumbled cement showed the red of bricks. And the old man had opened the door of the tower. A spade and a pickax were shining in the darkness therein, thrown down on top of one another in the form of a cross, and the weights of an old clock were dangling there, almost to the ground, both hanging down from above; but the pendulum was swinging back and forth in the shadows, and silently, the man he had encountered reset the clock by raising the weights.

Seventy. Seven times he had opened his poor old hands very wide, with a beaming smile. Seventy years; he was seventy years old, and every day of his life, he had come with his big key to rotate the chain of the clock in order that it might live another day.

And as Raymondin, his heart touched, made the gesture of taking the old man's hands in his own, he perceived that he had disappeared. He was no longer on the pathway of thistles himself, by in front of an immense wheat-field on the other side of the wall.

There were large brown ears extending their immobile heads to infinity against a sky violet-tinged by heat. They seemed to be aflame in the intense ardor, and extending before the young man's eyes like a sheet of incandescent metal. And a scythe was flying over the ears, as shiny and glittering as a crow's wing, and that wing was sweeping and swerving in the hand of an invisible reaper; but the ears were being laid down in sheaves beneath the flight of the scythe, and Raymondin was afraid.

The scythe worked for a long time, silently, and Raymondin suddenly saw the reaper who was maneuvering it.

Draped in light as if in a shroud, it was a tragic skeleton, an agile and restless skeleton whose shiny skull was crowned by immortelles; and cornflowers and poppies were laughing gaily between his femurs.

The gold of the wheat directly behind it shone a kind of light between its vertebrae, and Raymondin recognized the reaper: Death, the good worker, the Death that reaps silently, whose mission is always beautiful, because it reaps in large swathes.

A horror had gripped the young man's throat on seeing the reaper, like an automaton, toiling frenetically in the midst of the brown wheat, active in the sunlit silence of the countryside, when, all of a sudden, near the skeleton, a handsome nude adolescent surged forth.

As naked as beauty, as naked as the morning, as naked as ignorance, with a golden sickle in his hand, Amour—for it was him—collected the flowers, and with birdsong in his mouth, like the song of a skylark; and his mouth, red with the moist redness of the heart of a fruit, into which the teeth put nacre, sometimes brushed the calyx of a flower.

Amour collected and kissed the cornflowers, which are as blue as the gazes of young women; he gleaned and kissed the poppies, which are as red as wounds; and, strange to relate, beneath his golden sickle the stems of the cut flowers wept a sap warmer and more vermilion than the ears scythed by the hand of Death.

Death reaps and Amour gleans;
She in her great white shroud.
He with his fine young means

Marches alone and proud;
Marches and sings without fear
And death reaps before him
With her shiny bright scythe.

And as, unconsciously paralyzed by fear, Raymondin hummed the old song, the décor changed, the wheat vanished, and beneath a gray autumn sky, there were the interminable furrows of a long field of labor; and among the clods of earth protruding between the tufts of pale stubble, the erstwhile reaper reappeared, but this time steering a plough.

The skeletal reaper had become a laborer. A pale dusk enveloped him with a sad light; birds of passage were passing overhead, and on his heels, the handsome naked adolescent still marched; he marched with ears of wheat and cornflowers in his hair, proud of the last crop, with the same song on his lips; and in that dismal setting, he sowed, he sowed across the old furrows, and his divine gesture, his gesture of hope, filled the immense distress of the horizon with courage and new hope.

When Death labors, Amour sows.

And as Amour sang, Raymondin understood that it was no longer necessary to weep, for to love is to die and be reborn; that it was necessary not to be afraid to know his life, but to look it straight in the face and act in accordance with the vision of the day; that every minute lived belonged to the scythe of Death, as every intoxication passed under the sickle of Amour, and that their instruments of murder were, after all, only their wings.

41

Amour scythes with his wing.
With her wing, Death harvests.

And Raymondin found himself outside the little tower again, at the foot of the great white wall. The clock was still ticking noisily, but night had almost come, and Raymondin, shoving aside the thistles that had strangely grown during his dream, took the road to the town and the valley again.

THE OLD DUKE'S DAUGHTERS

A tale for Liane.[1]

S INCE dawn the governor's three daughters had been standing at the large window that overlooked the countryside, and the sun had already sunk into a heap of pink clouds and vanished from the horizon. In the vast room, hung with silken tapestries, a group of maidservants was gently tormenting the strings of theorbos and large archlutes and the entire octagonal courtyard was filled with a vague and delicate murmur, but the three sisters did not hear it. Their gazes, like their thoughts, were far beyond the crenellated ramparts of the city, far beyond the fields of rye and the vegetable gardens of the neighboring villages, gazes and thoughts fixed in the distance, a long way away, toward the blue mountains, into which, with their large-wheeled carts, their little thin horses with braided manes and their ragged bands of grimacing, thieving children, the last of the bohemians had just disappeared.

For a month they had been filing past, in groups of between twenty-five and a hundred companions, below

1 The dancer and courtesan "Liane de Pougy" (Anne-Marie Chassaigne, 1869-1950).

the city, well-guarded by its triple wall, with a clutch of curious heads at each crenellation. The three duchesses, even better guarded in the high citadel that their father governed, had seen more than one Lord of Egypt go by, on foot or on horseback, head held high and torso braced, with curly black hair and a bronzed face illuminated by large golden eyes. For a month, amused by the grimaces and the antics of the vagabonds, they had abandoned the balconied window of the room that overlooked the market square and faced the cathedral. They had adopted the double ogive of their oratory, and spent their beautiful mornings, their afternoons and their long evenings there, occupied in watching, on the road on the other side of the stagnant water of the moat, the metallic gazes and white-toothed smiles of the young bohemians.

And throughout the city, the women, wives of artisans or respectable townsfolk, were as curious as the duchesses about the Egyptian pagans. It was the same every spring, when the accursed riders of the Sabbat, pouring out of who knew where—the marches of Bulgaria or the provinces of Bohemia, or perhaps further away, who could tell?—flooded into the regions like a swarm of locusts, following in the footsteps, one might have thought, of their ancestor Attila. Their narrow Moorish faces and their long oblique eyes revolutionized the women; they quit the spinning-wheel and the distaff or the laundry-room, the church or the pantry, to go and crowd the ramparts, and there they nudged one another and laughed like ripe figs at the night of the bandits' naked children. Fortunate were the husbands when they did not venture out like loose women into the very heart of their encampments, amid the tents and the carts.

They, the miscreants, put the manors and the farms to pillage, allowing their horses to graze in the middle of the crops, slaughtering pigs in the sties and cockerels in the henhouses; told the fortunes of pregnant women who, in nine months, would give birth to Christians as dark as olives and as hairy as goats; sold young men philters to make young women fall in love; and tricked wives out of their husbands' money. In exchange for the good honest coin there was crude jewelry of beaten silver, rings for fastening shoulder-knots, securing fidelity, and amulets against mortal fevers; equivocal horoscopes drawn by the mouths of toothless old crones from the depths of cauldrons full of who knew what reeking broth, packets of dry herbs and lofty pronouncements of Master Albert extracted by means of Tarot cards, and a thousand other mummeries that melted the townspeople's solid wealth as if in a crucible, coin and gold alike disappearing into dressers and hidey-holes, flown away in a month, swallowed by the obscene purses of the louse-ridden bandits.

And it had been the same for years. Along with the first periwinkles on the banks, they appeared in the countryside, on horseback or on foot, famished and proud, with haversacks on their saddle-bows, cauldrons, iron forks and tin trays—all their fortune, in sum—on the bent backs of the women, the old heaped up with the naked children, like impure gods, in the carts; and all that rabble sang and danced with joy in the rain, the wind and the sun, scraping the guzla with light kicks of the heel that made them hop and pirouette, especially the beautiful girls, like so many sparks.

Their strident bursts of laughter and their crazy stamping put spells on the crossroads. As the first star lit up in the sky they began their oscillation, to continue it around the big fires well into the night, and the roads were no longer safe because of all those vagabonds roaming the region.

Finally, that spring, at the request of the aldermen and merchants, the Duke and governor had forbidden anyone to go out of the gates during the entire passage of the accursed pagans, and throughout the beautiful month of April they had filed past on the other side of the moat and camped under the ramparts, watched from the height of the round-paths and the watchtowers by the covetous eyes of the wives of townsmen and the daughters of artisans, all secretly aggrieved and resentful against the Duke and his edict.

Throughout the beautiful month of April, when the hawthorn is in flower and the country roads are embalmed by apple-blossoms, with the sunlight everywhere, on the streams and pools, and the young shoots of the willows, it had been necessary for them to stay at home, sitting in the corner of the hearth, plying the needle or spinning wool instead of running through the meadows picking primroses—and the consternation was in the noble houses of the city as well as the hovels of the outlying districts.

It was also in the palace, to which the duchesses were accustomed to summon, once in the course of their passage, the finest musicians among the nomads, and listening all day long to their violins and their songs; but the inflexible Duke had forbidden the bohemians to enter the city, just as he had forbidden the inhabitants to go out to their carts and tents.

The young duchesses had conceived a resentment against their father, which increased day by day and the hordes of Egypt thinned out, becoming sparser on the roads; for a rumor had spread, coming from the surrounding countryside and now circulating in the city, that the bohemians, discontented with the ban, would make a long detour during their next passage, and would henceforth avoid the city with the closed gates, so this would be the last time that they would make camp in the shadow of its walls, and would never be seen again.

It was already two days since the last cart of the last tribe had plunged slowly into the golden haze of the dusk and the blue of the landscape with the diabolical twanging of guitars and the gambols of naked children. Since then there had been silence, only troubled by the chirping of birds, the crushing silence of the fields, only relieved by the swish of the reapers' scythes; and the deserted road, snaking away and diminishing over the leagues, with the dark patch of the occasional pedestrian, with the semblance of an ant; and, in the distance, far away, the sentinel mountains, standing out immutably against the pale sky, guarding the horizon.

It was the third evening, and since dawn, the governor's three daughters had been standing at the open window overlooking the fields, and in the vast room, filled a little while ago by the muffled chatter and song of the maidservants, the theorbos and the archlutes had fallen silent; for it was already two hours since the sun had sunk behind the violet summits, and the rising moon, finally emerging from the little cypress wood, was bathing the pale tapestries of the ducal gynaeceum with quicksilver. The three sisters had remained standing there by themselves, the meal time having drawn the maidservants to the kitchens.

The eldest of the duchesses, whose name was Bellangère and who was very pale, very tall and very serious, with chestnut-colored hair and beautiful dark eyes, slowly turned to her sisters, the blonde Yveline and the red-haired Mérilde, and without saying a word, with a finger over her mouth, she made a mysterious sign to them; and they were both gripped by a tremor, went pale and huddled closer to her. The sound of a provocative and charming viol sang gaily in the countryside, followed by a voice—but a voice of dream, so pure, alluring and sad was it, a voice of a spring, a voice of the moon, a voice of a flower that must weep in order to sing—and the two young women, lowering their heads meekly, followed their sister.

They went down into the high-ceilinged room with the blazoned vaults where their father was eating supper, plunged to the neck in a massive chair, by the light of wax candles suspended from the wall. He was supping there, the muzzles of his great danes posed on his knees, and armed valets corseted and coiffed in iron were ranged around him, awaiting his orders.

They came in like three enchantresses, and the gloomy old room brightened as if by an aurora, for they were almost naked in long rustling silken dresses laden with precious stones, and their hair, anointed with perfumes, Mérilde's red and Yvelaine's blonde, shone like flames outside the borders of pearls and brocade bonnets.

They leaned their bosoms and their breasts on the black of the chair, passed their naked arms around the Duke's neck and, holding themselves tightly against him in suppliant poses, smiling, with teasing fingers and caressing words, filled his tankard with a beverage that the silent Bellangère had brought. They moistened their pink lips with it playfully, and then, with a thousand kisses, Yvelaine, on her knees before her father, and Mérilde, half-sitting on the arm of the chair, compelled the Duke to take three draughts, while Bellangère, her amphora in her hand, stood directly behind him.

And when the Duke became drowsy, the tankard circulated around the table. The delicate hands of the duchesses offered it to the captains and the soldiers, and their eyes lit up under the rude iron helmets, and the scars brightened in the corners of their temples or on their cheeks, rendering the faces mask-like; for the young duchesses, their shoulders springing forth from their corsages, were laughing with their lips and their eyes at the valets as at the lords, applying their white fingers to the mouths, and, amid the bold gestures and sketches of embraces, truly had the appearance of three young courtesans.

In the distance, in the limpid night, the viol was still singing, the voice still weeping.

And gradually, all the men-at-arms in the Duke's retinue became drowsy; they snored, some with their heads on the table and others slumped in a corner of the hall, and in the bodyguard, the sentinels were also asleep, intoxicated by the passage of the three duchesses, and throughout the citadel a muted rumble was audible; a magic sleep kept all the men unconscious.

In the distance, far away, in the iridescent clearings, the luminous pathways and the bright undergrowth of the moonlit forest, there was the whinnying and the sonorous gallop of three horses scurrying away—giddy up!—through the trees, and there was a noise of breaking branches, and in a frightened whisper of young leaves, the chirping of birds awakened in passage, the little cries of anxious chicks—but a joyful voice, a voice that was no longer plaintive, reassured the braches, the nests and the foliage, and the songs and laughter of three other voices responded to that voice, like trills.

And when dawn broke upon the Ducal castle, the maidservants stopped, bewildered, on the threshold of the gynaeceum: the three duchesses had disappeared. The postern that opened to the countryside was found wide open, with the sentinel still standing beside it, his torso leaning on the arch, with a dagger in his heart. Had he been stabbed by one of the three young women, Bellangère, Yvelaine or Mérilde? An unknown hand had suspended a bohemian guzla and a sprig of broom, like a challenge, from the blazon of the gate.

All the men of the garrison, mobilized, scoured the countryside in vain; no trace was ever found of the duchesses, and never again did the band of bohemians pass the city.

Since the nascent dawn, the Duke's three daughters had been standing at the window.

MELUSINE ENCHANTED

*S*O *sweetly she intoxicated gazes,*
    Resplendent with a purity so divine
    That her people expelled her from her city.
The beautiful Melusine;
Because of her eyes, the color of aquamarine,
The roseate fires of her breast
And her beautiful red hair
Scattered over her long neck.

For a long time, far from the towns
That surrounded the ramparts,
Through the forest wandered
The beautiful Melusine;
Fearful and weeping, her brocade dress
Torn on the hawthorn thickets
And her bare feet bloodied in the thin grass
Of the clearings where roe deer gazed.

She reached the lands of enchantment thus
In the golden heaths green with holly,
And there her blue eyes saw that the wolves

Followed her in a troop
And the errant clouds and the moon,
And even the long-eared owls
Stopped in the heavens when she
Paused in the russet fields. . . .

Raymondin de Lusignan woke up.

The little wood of ash-trees where he had gone to sleep was weeping softly in the rain, and on the mist-drowned horizon, the heathlands extended as far as the eye could see. The singing voice had fallen silent, and as far as his gaze could reach, there was silence and solitude.

For how many hours had he been sleeping in that arbor in the wild wood, and what had become of the members of his retinue? A great disturbance stirred within him, and he felt his arms and sides curiously, his temples moist with sweat, unknowingly glad of the rain.

So sweetly she intoxicated gazes,
Resplendent with a purity so divine
That her people expelled her from her city.
The beautiful Melusine . . .

The song pursued him, and, his fingers having encountered the ivory horn hanging from his belt, he now remembered having traversed the heath in bright sunlight, under the glare of midday. A strange torpor, an irresistible pressure, had gripped him, and he had yielded to it, since he found himself sitting here, seven hours later, in the dusk, his head bare under the downpour and his heart obsessed by a name that he had never heard before.

Melusine! Melusine! That name, so sweet that it seemed to caress the lips like lips, and intoxicate thought like a philter. . . .

He was, however, quite alone; there was no one in the ten leagues of gorse and fleeting heather, gray in the rain, extending to the hills that closed the horizon, but the song was still buzzing in his ears, the song and the musical voice that was singing it.

At that moment, with an abrupt flutter of wings, a rook flew over his head, and Lusignan then remembered a little old woman, ragged and wrinkled, encountered gathering dry branches from the mossy feet of the ash-trees, at the moment that he had entered the wood.

An old crone at midday, a rook at dusk!

Lusignan, a great hunter of wolves and killer of wild boar, knew exactly how to recite in Latin an *Ave* and a *Pater*; he pronounced them at that moment, suspecting in his long sleep some entrapment of the fays. Do legends not make them dance by night in the violently scented air of the heather and the gorse, as in the moonlit mists of ponds?

And, having crossed himself three times, the Comte got to his feet, shook the residual rain from his crimson bliaut with a shrug of the shoulders, and, taking his bearings from the last gleams of the setting sun, strode straight ahead through the heather in the direction of his burg.

"And the jealous fays have changed her into a serpent; her imperious beauty, which charmed the birds in the sky and the errant beasts in the woods, frightens the solitudes today.

"Transformed into a monstrous hydra, she sleeps all day in the sun, coiled up in the russet grass of the heath; by night she crawls sadly over the pebbles of dry streambeds silvered by the moonlight, and her regretful hissing awakens echoes from ravine to ravine.

"Where is that? Far away and close at hand, here and there, in the land of the fays, who watch over their prisoner invisibly, in the golden heaths, made verdant by the holly, which you have traversed a hundred times without suspecting the malign ladies laughing in the brushwood, sitting around you in a circle.

"In the land of the fays, where the ensorcelled hydra has been waiting for a hundred years for the bold knight who, gripping her head in both hands, will dare to kiss her viscous lips, where death resides.

"The jealous fays have changed her into a serpent; her imperious beauty, which charmed the birds in the sky and the errant beasts in the woods, frightens the solitudes today.

"Only the lips of a man can break the enchantment, but for the promised hero, the hydra is still waiting. When, in the russet heather, overwhelmed by the heat, will the lethargic serpent rear up on her tail, hissing, to be gripped around the neck by her liberator? When will the virgin, finally liberated, spring forth, as naked as a pearl and as white as foam, from the scales of the monster?

"The charm is in the beauty that slumbers, captive in the squamous and noisy sheath of the hydra; deliverance is in the kiss of the hero with a soul sufficiently tempered to drink the poison and confront death.

"To him the power and numerous lineage, to him fortune and renown; he will found a heroic and princely house."

And the voice died away, as if stifled by the thickness of the wall. Raymondin, who was asleep, his arms crossed over his breast, in the big oak bed blazoned with his arms, raised himself up on his elbow, moist with sweat. That voice of dream had not pronounced a name, and yet a conviction gripped him that the song was speaking of Melusine, Melusine still and Melusine forever. He pricked up his ears and, thinking that he could hear voices whispering under the window, he got up, ran barefoot over the tiles to the narrow casement overlooking the open country, and opened the panel. Outside, dawn had scarcely broken: a wan, cold dawn of the end of October, a shroud of mist floating over the valley, reminiscent of a sea of vapors, with a few hilltops emerging here and there, half-shadowed.

And Lusignan, having leaned out, perceived a kind of beggar standing in the mist, at the foot of the seigneurial keep, with his beard and hair braided like that of bohemians. With copper loops in his ears, draped in a mantle of broad-striped fabric, he was leaning on a staff and, his eyes sparkling under bushy eyebrows, he was muttering, his mouth full of confused words, and seemed by his gestures to be negotiating with soldiers that he, Lusignan, could not see, but assumed to be the guards at the postern.

Lusignan called out and ordered that the old man should be brought to him straight away. His squire came back almost immediately, head bowed; he had not seen anyone at the foot of the keep. Monseigneur must have been the victim of some dream; the sentinel on duty at the postern of the burg had not seen anyone at all since the previous evening.

Chagrined, Raymondin returned to the window. The equivocal beggar with the braided beard was no longer there; a vision of the early morning, he had vanished into the mist.

It was then that the mild lord fell into a profound melancholy.

From that day on, everything that had interested him before—the handling of arms, shooting with the bow, jousting with the lance, and even the pleasures of the hunt, whether hunting with falcons in the meadows or beating the profound forests for deer and wild boars, everything that had once been the joy of his life, suddenly ceased to occupy him.

He wandered all day long, depressed and dismal, through the countryside, inattentive to the footfalls of his mare, letting her wander at random through the brushwood and the crops, more like a phantom riding in expiation some beast of dream than an honest and loyal knight.

In the evenings he returned, harassed, and sat down without unsealing his lips at the seigneurial table, where he no longer listened to the chaplain's *Benedictus*. On Sundays, he scarcely went to church. He was no longer able either to kneel, or to sit down, and his friends no longer recognized him. He became thin, haggard and pale, and let his hair and beard grow; they spilled out from beneath his helmet, dusty and bushy. By night, he got up with a start, to stride, in the wind and the rain, along the round-path of the ramparts. One might have thought that he was listening to voices, and the sentinels feared seeing him pass close by at midnight, muttering confused words. In the vicinity, the opinion was affirmed that bohemians had cast a spell on him.

A year from then, on a sultry day in August, as he was coming back at dusk from one of the distant aimless excursions with which he now consumed his life, his mare, whose bridle he had allowed to rest on her neck, as usual, made an abrupt somersault, which woke him from his torpor. He stood up in the saddle and opened his eyes wide.

A few paces in front of him, in the vast bare plain, three women—or, rather, three female forms—were agitating, seemingly dancing around a great fire of dry grass. With the look of old beggar-women clad in singularly luminous rags, they were shaking thin bare arms frenetically above the flames, and with bursts of wild laughter, which were not so much audible as divined by the contortions of their bodies, they were whirling in the smoke, as if transparent, even brighter than the atmosphere of the bright summer's day, the color of amber against the inflamed redness of the evening.

They pronounced his name three times, and evaporated in the air—and Lusignan thought about the little old lady in the ash-wood, and then the bohemian beggar glimpsed at dawn at the postern of the burg.

But who was the third? For he had certainly recognized the other two, but what he did not recognize and was frightened not to be able to recognize, was the locality into which his mare had brought him. Those undulations of the terrain, those meager trees at ground level and that chain of mountains on the horizon were unknown to him.

A great sadness gripped him in that hostile solitude. He was no longer in the immense plain of a little while before; he had before him an uncultivated and ravined heath, florid with dwarf thistles and tall flowering mallows, with the debris of a temple scattered here and there, and stumps of columns strewing the terrain. And although there was not a breath of wind in the air, the faded rosy mallows and the hostile thistles quivered sadly under a red and green sky: the red of blood and the green of wounds.

He urged his mount forward, but this time his mare refused to obey, and Lusignan, having leaned forward to see the obstacle, perceived the serpent at her feet.

Gold-speckled green in hue, which became blue underneath, the hydra was asleep, coiled up on a bed of dry leaves; its triangular and fabulously small head was agape, showing in its black maw a triple row of sharp teeth, and six heavy necklaces of precious stones embraced it at intervals, to indicate that it was of royal birth. Its head reposed on a large crimson lily, and Lusignan, having dismounted and attached his mare to a nearby cypress, approached it stealthily.

Abruptly, he seized the serpent by the head, and lifted it with all the strength of his arms to the level of his lips, and, in spite of his disgust, applied his mouth to the mouth of the monster.

Suddenly awakened, with a shrill hiss, the hydra had coiled itself furiously around the gentle lord. It had enlaced the man, and was crushing his ribs with all the weight of its rings; it held his feet tight with its tail, and froze his abdomen with the cold of its scales.

And under the frightful embrace, and the forked tongue that darted forth menacingly, the oppressed warrior fainted; and, frozen, drank with avid lips the drool and venom of the monster. He drank them three times.

Then, through the solitude, the high mallows rustled madly, and the thistles were ignited with a metallic gleam. With a long, long cry, the liberated virgin had surged naked from the hideous envelope and thrown her arms around the neck of her conqueror; then, suddenly, she had lowered her eyes, her large eyes the color of shadow, and became entirely pink, roseate from the toenails of her naked feet to the fresh eglantine of her breasts.

Melusine was ashamed, seeing that she had no garment.

Lusignan then threw his warrior's mantle over the splendid nudity of the virgin and, kissing her pouting lips, sat her on the rump behind him. The mare whinnied, and, vibrant with desire, his heart inundated with delight, the proud lord carried his blushing prey away through the pink heather of the landscape that had become familiar once again.

In the brushwood, the voices of the fays sang: "To Lusignan power and a numerous lineage! To Lusignan a warrior and royal house!"

The sun, completely set, had disappeared from the horizon, but one last oblique ray illuminated, like a golden dot, the russet hair of Melusine, going on the rump behind her master to found the race of the Lusignans.

MANDOSIANE CAPTIVE

PRINCESS MANDOSIANE was six hundred years old. For six centuries she had lived, embroidered in velvet with a face and hands of painted silk. She was entirely clad in pearls, with a necklace so heavy with embroidery that it bulged, and the arabesques of her robe, woven in silver fabric, were of the most delicate golden thread.

An ultramarine mantle patterned with anemones was fastened over her breast by veritable precious stones, and sapphire cabochons ornamented the hem of her dress.

She had figured for a long time in processions and royal fêtes. She was brought out then, hoisted on a flagpole, and the glitter of her jewels delighted queens and common folk. They were happy times, when, through the paved streets, beneath the flutter of flamboyant pennants, the Princess Mandosiane was acclaimed. Then she was returned ceremoniously to the treasure of the cathedral and she was shown to foreigners in exchange for copious gold.

There was no marvel like that miraculous Princess. She was born of the dream and the obstinate toil of twenty nuns, who, for fifty years, had labored extracting the delightful and hieratic figure from skeins of silk and silver.

Her hair was yellow silk; two tourmalines of the most beautiful blue had been incrusted at the location of her irises, and she was holding a sheaf of white velvet lilies, placed over her heart.

Then the era of processions passed; thrones were abolished; kings disappeared; civilization made progress; and the princess of pearls and painted silk remained confined henceforth to the shadow of the cathedral.

She spent her days there in the half-light of a crypt, with a heap of bizarre things grimacing in the corners. There were ancient statues, tankards beside ciboria, old church ornaments, copes still stiff, as if gilded by the sun, slowly fading away in the night, with the chalices that were no longer used by officiants. There was also an old Christ backed up in a corner, completely veiled in spiders' webs.

The door of the subterranean chapel was never opened. All those old things lay dormant there, buried and forgotten. And a great despair gripped the heart of Princess Mandosiane

She lent her ear to the counsel of the red mouse, an insidious little mouse, as quick as lightning, tenacious and willful, which had already been pestering her for years.

"Why are you obstinate in remaining a captive, trussed up in all the pearls and embroideries that wrap you? It's no life, yours. You've never lived, even in the times when you were resplendent beneath the blue sky of carilloned fêtes, acclaimed by the intoxication of crowds, and now, you see, it's oblivion and death. If you wanted, with my sharp teeth, I'd loosen one by one the silken stitches and the golden cord that have held you in place, motionless, for six hundred years, in that shiny velvet—which, between us, no longer has much of a gleam.

"It might perhaps cause you a little pain, especially when I pick out stitches close to the heart, but I'd begin with the long contours, those of the hands and the face, and you'd already be able to stretch and move, and you'd see how good it is to breathe and live! Beautiful as you are, with your face of a folktale princess, and rich with the fabulous treasure with which your garment is respondent, you'd be dressed by the greatest designers; you'd be taken for the daughter of a banker, and marry, at the very least, a French prince.

"You have millions in pearls on you! Come on, let me set you free; you'll revolutionize the world.

"If you only knew how good it is to be free, to breathe in the wind, filling your lungs, and follow your own whim! You're decked out in those opals and sapphires like a knight in armor, and you've never even fought in battle. I know the roads that lead to the land of Wellbeing. Let yourself blossom outside your embroidered sheath; we'll go around the world together and I promise you a throne and the love of a hero."

Princess Mandosiane consented. The little red mouse immediately commenced its murderous work; his teeth sawed, cut and filed away the velvet eaten by mites; pearls tinkled as they fell, one by one, and on moonlit nights as in beautiful sunlit skies, in the crypt illuminated by a ventilation shaft, the red mouse cut and ate, always busy.

When it attacked the famous necklace of nacre and pearls, Princess Mandosiane had the sensation of a sharp coldness in her heart.

For several days already she had felt shivery and lighter, and, singularly supple in the midst of all those broken stitches, she undulated in the fabric as if animated by a breeze, and waited, delightedly, for the mouse to finish its work.

When the rodent's teeth sank into her bosom, the poor princess of spangles and silk, this time, collapsed entirely. There was something like a stream of ashes on the flagstones of the obscure chapel, the soft fall of fleecy silks, dismantled braid and luminous rags; a few cabochons rolled away like grains of wheat, and the old mite-ridden velvet of the banner tore from top to bottom.

Thus died Princess Mandosiane, for having listened to the insidious advice of a little mouse.

ORIANE VANQUISHED

Oriane the fay was the shepherd's alarm
Vaguely glimpsed in her blue-tinted rooms,
She put to sleep, weary and charmed
Knights helmed with eagle's plumes.

THE moon penetrated into the cavern, spangling the mica-incrusted walls of rock with blue-tinted gleams. A moving cascade of ivy obstructed the entrance, dotted here and there with large clematis flowers, like stars: an inextricable and supple mesh of foliage and corollas, through which the clearing of the forest appeared, all white with the flickering light of the star on the pale tops of the chestnut trees.

Supported by three pillars of basalt, the grotto was sunk in a half-light of dream, invaded on all sides by mistletoe, honeysuckle and tall ferns whose dentellate leaves shone strangely; everywhere, from fissures in the vaults, and crevices in the pillars and the ground, vegetation had sprouted. There were brambles, eglantines, trailing hops, foaming hemlock and broad burdocks with glaucous velvet leaves; and all of that as entangled, climbing and falling back, plants gripping one another and crawling over the moss, palpitating vaguely with the tremor of stems and the vitality of sap, under the blue moonlight slipping in from outside.

Sometimes, in the chestnuts of the clearing, a slight

noise whispered, which was the respiration of the dormant forest; then the breeze went further, to torment a few nests in the thickets, and a great whinnying tore through the silence; a herd of wild horses passed by at a gallop, their rumps shiny in the moonlight filtering between the mobile leaves.

The forest was full of those herds of mares and unbroken stallions; they furrowed it in all directions, with a loud noise of broken branches. They wandered at random, their breasts white with foam and their manes flying, assembled around the oldest stallion of the herd, and, on spring nights, in the mating season, they fought furiously until dawn, biting one another in the belly and whinnying; the nests in the bushes were alarmed, and the roe deer in the thickets; and the forest was impenetrable because of the innumerable wild horses that guarded it, prompt to charge any human being and trample him.

In the cavern, the brambles and the tall ferns continued to slumber, and silver droplets pearled on the moonlit honeysuckle leaves. In the mesh of ivy, the clematis flowers seemed to open more widely; and bloomed like shiny flakes of frost in the clumps of brambles, under which red-gold and steely glimmers now lit up; and from the tangle of thorns and burdocks sprang a magical efflorescence of épées.

There were Celtic swords with enormous hilts, Gothic two-edged swords, all straight, Saracen swords with curved blades, Anglo-Saxon lances, and even medieval Frankish spears. Also surging forth here and there amid the branches, as if left behind after a battle, were the drawn bows, quivers and pointed arrows of hostile flowers, and in the brambles were now swinging bucklers and helmets, which reflected the moonlight like mirrors; the petals of charmed eglantines were detached there, and beneath that iron flora, the faces of sleeping warriors slowly emerged, ecstatic in the shadows. Clean-shaven craniums and heavy blond curls, the snub-nosed profiles and fleshy smiles of bold pagans with bronzed skin, the long eyelids allowing blue gazes to filter through, forever immobile, of some son of the Norman race, the thickset shoulders of warrior Goths, the thin and muscular torsos of Saxon cavaliers, the white beards of old campaigners and the beardless, pink faces, almost angelic, of young pages, there were a good hundred of them asleep there in the grotto with metallic reflections, beneath the steel flora of their arms, captives forever of the ice and the brambles, knights and barons, paladins and pirates, Christian kings and miscreant dogs, blond-haired ephebes and aged equerries: the same dream enchanted their closed eyes and haloed their faces with ecstasy.

Extended in their various poses, some lying on their backs, others face down with their heads under their arms, all had retained the same gesture of adoration and delirious prayer, for all their hands were joined, and one sensed that they must all have fallen asleep with their eyes fixed on the same vision, with their lips imploring same name: *Oriane*.

And now, finally evoked and rendered tangible by the desire of her lovers, Oriane appears in person in the shadows of the ensorcelled grotto, and illuminates it with her presence.

Standing in an aureole of milky and quivering gleams, like the halo that circles the moon on rainy nights, she leans the nudity of a fay on the transparent fractures of a cathedral of ice; stalactites surround her and three crystal steps display their glaucous humidity at her feet. Everything about her has reflections of snow and nacre; the pale and heavy hair that hangs down to her heels has the imperceptible hint of gold with which the fires of dawn brush the frost, and her entire naked body shines like a pearl, a fabulous pearl that the orient has painted pink, sparkling from the nipples of her breasts, the nails of the big toes and the tips of the fingers, enlivening their rosiness, to the flowering rose that opens at the location of her lips, where lies the kiss.

Captive of their desires, as they are captives of her beauty; Oriane arches her back and moves slowly beneath her moonlit mane, stretching voluptuously, and then leans, dazzled, toward a small oval mirror that she holds in one hand, a mysterious opal in the depths of which the prayerful faces of each of the warriors appear, one by one.

For how many years has Oriane retained them, motionless and mute, retrenched from life, almost turned to phantoms in the brambles and hemlock of her lair? Some a hundred years, others only fifty; there are some there who have been asleep for twenty winters, others for a month. There is an entire century of amour and reckless covetousness asleep there, in the depths of the forest, vaguely appeased in a dream that suppresses the world for them but forbids them death.

Each of those who lies dormant there, ecstatic, with

hands clasped, arrived on some fine April morning or lukewarm autumn evening, helmet on the head and hope in the heart, to knock with the flat of his blade on the threshold of the cavern; there they have dismounted, tied their horse to some holm-oak, and then, stammering words of amour, entered.

And the weary horse, tired of waiting, after having stripped the foliage from the trees and the grass from the ground, has broken its tether and fled into the forest, becoming wild again, and, the mare of the adolescent having encountered the palfrey of the knight there, the herds of mares and stallions now gallop, whinnying, their rumps shiny in the moonlight, through the nocturnal forest, awakening the loud breakage of dead branches.

On this beautiful night in July, in the midst of the reverie of the forest in flower and the slumbering adoration of her lovers, Oriane is sad; in the distance the herds of mares have whinnied loudly, she knows that the forest is no longer impenetrable and that times have changed. An incorruptible hero, brought up by monks in the hatred and horror of women, a proud adolescent with a grim heart and pure hands has just entered it. He has already crossed the edge of the forest and, firm in the saddle, helmed and armored in mat silver, sad and sullen beneath the moon, sullen itself, he is advancing slowly but surely through the short grass of the pathways and the wild oats of the clearings, the embalmed clearings of her forest, where the bees will no longer flutter at midday and the dragonflies at dusk, for the cruel ephebe is bringing deliverance in his right hand and death in his left.

Deliverance for them, death for her—worse than death; old age that is the real death of women and fays, since it extinguishes amour and destroys desire.

And Oriane leans over to smile one last time at the opal mirror that is already becoming tarnished; and yet, what has she done to those monks? She, the charm and enchantment of gazes and the joy of nature, how radiant she has been, corolla, vibrant wind or woman, what has she done for anyone to excite this harsh conqueror? The times have changed, and against him, all her traps will be vain! Oriane knows that in advance, for he is coming towards her, hardened by hatred and ablaze with rancor, an avenger and administrator of justice.

He detested and abhorred her beauty, which had made the others slaves, and it is not so much to liberate them as to punish her that he had made this perilous voyage, for in the depths of his heart, he is scornful of those heroes that a woman had been able to vanquish, and his hatred for her was further exasperated by his scorn for their laxity; and the cruel adolescent was getting closer by the hour. A complicit owl was guiding him through the woods, flying before him from tree to tree.

Standing on her throne of ice, in the depths of her grotto, Oriane could hear the frightful nocturnal bird ululating; she heard branches drawing aside, the pommel of the sword bumping against the saddle; and every footfall of the horse resounded in her heart.

To be sure, she would have been able to lead him astray by means of subtle mirages, illusions and vain appearances, slowing down his progress through sudden inextricable thickets and unexpected marshes; she could have hidden herself in some fleeting form, a wild animal, bird or flower, but what would be the point? Times had changed; she was vanquished in advance. It was Christ who was marching with that child, Christ the enemy of joy, sensuality and amour. He it was who had excited against her that executioner with the visage of an archangel—and now two tears were pearling in the pale eyes of the fay, and the shiny face of her mirror was entirely tarnished.

The sweet Oriane knew that she was defenseless; she loved her vanquisher.

At that moment, an immense light irrupted into the grotto. With the trenchant edge of his blade a man had just ripped through the moving curtain of ivy that guarded the threshold.

As if laminated with silver by the moon, a slender silhouette loomed up against the clearing, a helmeted silhouette, on which a living owl perched on the summit deployed two great wings: Amadis.

Then, having put his aurochs-horn trumpet to his mouth, Amadis blew three times with all the force of his lungs, and, taking his épée by the blade, holding it like a cross in front of him, he came into the lair.

"By the omnipotent Christ and Our Lady the Virgin, let the scales fall from the eyes that the Accursed One has troubled, and let the Christian heroes retained asleep by the weight of her spells rise to their feet, finally free."

And, the bodies lying there having risen to their feet, with a great clanking of iron, Amadis saw that, beneath their rust and disjointed armor, the beings that appeared among the flowers and the plants all had the green-tinted faces of cadavers or gleaming skeletons—and he could not help stepping back.

With a sinister rattle of tibias hooked on to femurs, fleshy chard scraping with a soft sound in the grip of clenched desiccated fingers, and a nauseating odor of carrion, the atrocious vision only lasted for a moment. After a vain struggle to stand upright, the larvae of the knights had fallen back into the brushwood; now the cadavers were slowly liquefying. Amadis' exorcism had only awakened the putrefaction of those who had long been prey to the worms, and the broken spell had allowed, like a broken dyke, a humanity ripe for the tomb to flow freely. One alone, a skeleton, remained propped in a sitting position, sniggering mute laughter in a ray of moonlight, its vertebrae caught in a flowering eglantine.

Standing in the middle of the charnel-house, Amadis felt mortally sad.

Then Oriane said: "What good has your courage done? They were dreaming, and living their dreams. That one knew full well what he was doing in bringing you here." And with her tremulous and wrinkled hand, which had already become the hand of an old woman, the fay pointed at the owl. "You have prepared his pasture for him."

Then Amadis looked at her. Poor Oriane! Her hair had become gray, and, shriveled, toothless, coughing, bent double and broken, looking like a specter herself with her skin the color of ash and her eyes white with cataracts between bloody lids, Oriane, that nudity nacreous as a pearl a little while before, extended a long Sibylline arm toward the hero and in a doleful voice, said:

"And me, what have I done? I had the age of their illusions, and their desires made me young. Beautiful in their amour, I smiled at their dream and my smile protected them against death by smiling at them. Today, the number of years forgotten in my presence and the weight of their regret is overwhelming me; their awakening has aged me by a thousand years, and now I am condemned to live for a thousand years, hideous and sad, the life that each of them might have lived down here. Oh, misfortunate child, the last illusion that those men still had, flourished in these woods, and it is you who have killed it."

In the time required to hear that, she had vanished.

In the clearing, day was breaking. A sad light illuminated the cadavers heaped pell-mell in the grotto, and, perched on the head of a dead man, the owl was digging curiously with his beak in the place where two eyes once full of azure had been, now two black and filthy holes.

NEIGHILDE

After Andersen.

NEIGHILDE *sometimes travels far.*
A sleigh lined with frost
Carries her above the clouds
Toward kinder climes.

Like a dot amid the clouds
Streaking through snowy skies
Above the flocks of cranes
Neghilde's misty sleigh is seen.

Old wolves sitting in the snow
Howling in deserted woods
And crows from her cortege,
Crying hunger, crying winter.

Through the wind and the squalls
She goes with frosty fingers
To pick great bizarre flowers
Whose petals are stars.

A child abed in an attic
Frozen by fear in his sheets
Thinks Neighilde is watching him
But she does not even see him.

She is out there in Norway
Far beyond the seas
In an eternal place of snow
Where future winters sleep.

Little Peter was asleep in the icy splendor of Neig-hilde's palace, in the middle of the festival hall, frozen in the transparency of an enormous pillar. He was asleep there, curled up, his fur bonnet pulled down over his eyes, his little hands plunged into his mittens, having become a very little thing, like a relic in a glass case. Around him there was bleak enchantment, all pallors and pink gleams, all the stalactites and the icebergs of the palace illuminated by an aurora borealis; other rooms opened to infinity, despairingly vast and empty, and also despairingly white; the polar wind blew there like a mad thing, and night and day the snowflakes fluttered there, chased and driven into the corners by the gusts of the north wind.

They were the guardians of the palace. Lying in ambush on the thresholds; with their cutting breath they prevented the snow and ice from walling up the doorways; and like an immense madrepore, a thousand needles of ice tapering in the night, rigid and gigantic, rich with all the fires and changing reflections of the rainbow, spectral and splendid, Neighilde's palace was as flamboyant as a prism in the midst of the silence and the polar ice heaped up by winter.

Eternal winter, eternal distress, eternal blaze of the night ignited by the boreal dawns—and little Peter lived in that distress, in that solitude and silence, black and stiff with cold under his abrasive furs, but insensible to suffering, having become an icicle himself since Neighilde had passed her frosty hand over his heart, indifferent to everything, in truth, hallucinated by the splendor of the vast dazzling empty rooms and the alarming vertigo of their vaults, full of darkness and stars.

How many years had he been there? Little Peter no longer knew. He had lost the notion of time in losing his memory.

By touching his heart, Neighilde had extinguished all flame in him; he no longer remembered the town in Norway where he had played as a child in the great square, resounding with the crack of whips and cries; he no longer remembered the old suburb with its gloomy streets, so narrow that the poor folk in the attics went to visit one another over bridges of planks extended from one house to another. In that city and in that suburb, however, on the fifth floor of an old artisanal house, lived an old grandmother with a quavering voice, whom little Peter had known intimately: a good old grandmother with white hair, who, in the long gray days of winter, spindle in hand, recounted legends to two small children crouching at her feet by the hearth, who already loved one another amorously.

Little Peter had been one of those children. Little Peter had lived for a long time in the distant and populous town in Norway resounding with the crack of whips and cries. A child swathed in furs like other children, he had often scampered over the great square, cluttered with sleighs during the winter months; but Peter had forgotten his name and the name of the grandmother, and the name of the street, and the name of the town where the snow fell for six months of the year out of twelve, speckling the gray uniformity of the sky with soft whiteness.

Oh, the white swarm of the big snowflakes in the mute air, always falling thicker, always denser! With what curiosity he had watched them dance in those days, his nose stuck to the panes of the little window, in the abode of the good grandmother: that little window, florid in June with the sweet-peas and nasturtiums, florid with frost in winter!

The old grandmother's stories called those clustered snowflakes white bees, saying that those bees had a queen, just like the golden bees of summer, but that she was a queen of ice, with frozen moonbeams on her shoulders by way of wings, and a long mantle of furry frost and misty snow; that her hive was beyond the pole and that it was a dismal motionless palace built of ice-floes, all pallors and splendors: an enormous spectral palace with vast deserted rooms, dazzling transparent and rigid cupolas, eternally illuminated by the aurora borealis.

That queen was named Neighilde, and little Peter loved and feared her. Oh, little Peter had loved that queen, petrified, like the lethargic bees of winter, that august virgin of the bleached visions of the pole, and had feared her simultaneously, very much, for the cracked voice of the grandmother had also made her restless and far-traveling, and on nights in December, it sometimes happened that, while looking up at the sky, one might see the Queen's sleigh appear there.

Oh, that Queen of the snows, with her cenacle of old wolves, sitting on the edges of fjords and howling mortally, with what delightful anguish and poignant terror she filled little Peter's soul in those days.

He was now her captive. By dint of loving her, he had attracted the dead gaze of the Queen, and Neighilde had wanted little Peter's soul for herself, and herself alone. Pressed to the royal breast, buried in the frost of a glacial bosom, Peter had known the torments and terrors of voyages through the clouds, above towns, straits and seas; great flocks of storks had fled before him; bands of witches had dispersed before him, screeching in the vapors of storms; sailors on ships had made the sign of the cross on seeing the spur of the sleigh that was carrying him past the sails.

He had seen the towers of cathedrals flee beneath his feet, gargoyles and belfries and gigantic gilded Saint Michaels blowing trumpets on top of campaniles, citadels on mountains, abbeys in valleys, rivers under bridges and other rivers through the fields; and always, great white bees whirling around them, high up in the pale sky; enormous crows flapping their wings around them, while in front of the sleigh two enormous white hens flew silently.

Little Peter had said a *Pater*, but Neighilde had kissed him on the forehead, and little Peter had forgotten his prayers, a great cold had gripped him, and, in pain, he had tried to call out to Gerda, the little girl who, in the old attic in the suburb, in the midst of the ashes of the hearth, had listened with him to the grandmother's tales; but Neighilde had placed her hand over Peter's heart, and Peter no longer remembered Gerda's name, nor the name of the grandmother, nor his own name, but he had suddenly stopped feeling cold. A sense of wellbeing had invaded him, and at the same time, the moon had flared up, as if it had grown more rounded amid the nacreous clouds, and Neighilde's mantle floated, immeasurably long, amid a denser flock of night-birds; and in the softness and the warmth, little Peter had gone to sleep.

He had not woken up since.

It was then that Gerda came into the hall. Gerda was the little girl who, on long summer evenings, sitting with Peter on the edge of the roof of their tall house, on a little bench fabricated for them and placed for them between the two windows, had watched swallows fly and honeysuckle petals flutter in the breeze.

Crouched at the grandmother's feet, she had listened more than once to the tale of Neighilde and believed, like Peter, in the existence of the white bees and frozen enchantment of Neighilde's palace far away beyond the pole, in the land of winter. She loved Peter amorously, and when he had disappeared she had set off in search of him, and in order to find him had left the town, the good grandmother in her attic, and the old abode in the suburb.

She had set forth singing a canticle, rich in the confidence of her brave little heart, and, in order to find her lost little friend, had interrogated the rivers and the reeds, the fields and the flowers, and in the immense monotonous and sad universe, she had walked for hours and days, months and years, without ever wearying, being still at the age of hope.

And nature and the sad universe had taken pity on the child. . . .

In order to take her to the land of the fays, a boat had detached itself from the river-bank; in order to let her pass, old twisted willows had suddenly straightened up; batrachian sorceresses had wished her good luck, and on one reputedly dangerous islet, an old women, something of a witch, agreeable and yet troubling, had welcomed her under an immense hood of yellow roses.

Gerda had even disarmed the fays. Under the golden comb that, in smoothing her hair, ought to have put her mind to sleep, she had retained her memory; flowers exiled in the depths of the earth had sprung forth under her tears, periwinkles had spoken and Gerda had learned from their corollas, which were mouths, where little Peter was hidden. And Gerda had resumed her route through the bleak and sad universe.

An old rook had served as her guide. Counseled by the bird, she had been able to please the son of a king, but she had also interested a princess and had been able to escape the perilous honor of the employment of favorite; the dreams she inspired had protected her flight, and as night fell she had been able to slip out of the palace—but other dangers awaited her, and other adventures.

Brigands had captured her in the nocturnal horror of a forest; she had been taken as a prisoner to their cavern, she had trembled under the knife of an ogress, but, miraculously saved by the daughter of a brigand, a frightful little savage entranced by her blue eyes and white skin, Gerda had regained her freedom and had reached the flat extent of the steppes on a reindeer's back, and the confines of Neighilde's realm.

She had wandered there for months under the low sky in the bitter wind, sent from hut to hut, recommended by Lapp sorceresses to Finnish sorceresses; then her faithful reindeer had been obliged to abandon her, as the old rook had done, and all alone, shivering in her crimson dress under her large swansdown bonnet, she had boldly penetrated into Neighilde's territory.

The Queen was then absent, summoned because of frost to Sicily, where the almond trees were in peril— she had gone to ensure the harvest—and in spite of the sentinel gusts at the doors, with their faces of frost and their cutting breath, Gerda had gone into the palace.

After the twentieth hall she found Peter asleep, captive in his pillar of ice, knelt down under the swirling snow, and softly intoned the canticle that they had once sung together in the attic with the little windows flowered with ice, in the old house in the suburb.

Christmas is flowering, white with white roses
And this is the advent of baby Jesus.

And the pillar split from top to bottom; little Peter slid out through the blue-tinted fissure, all the way to Gerda's feet, and she threw her arms around him.

Holly and mistletoe green branch to branch,
The humblest heads are these evening elect
Christmas is flowering, white with white roses
And this is the advent of baby Jesus.

And beneath the warmth of tears, the icicle in which little Peter's heat was frozen having melted, Peter woke up, recovered his memory, recognized Gerda, stammered a *Pater*, the name of the good grandmother and that of his town and that of his street, and, hand in hand with his little friend, fled Neighilde's palace at top speed.

Both of them reached the ice-sheet thus, and the steppe, and finally the fields, already green with the March barley, the fields already blue with the April periwinkles, and everywhere, along the route, the belfries of the villages repeated the divine canticle in humble refrain:

Hearts are flowering full of white roses
And this is the advent of baby Jesus.

PRINCESS NEIGEFLEUR

WHEN Queen Imogine found out that Princess Neigefleur was not dead, that the silken cord that she had tightened around her neck personally had only half-strangled her, and that the gnomes of the forest had placed that delicate body in a coffin of glass—and, what was worse, that they were keeping it invisible in a magic grotto—she went into a great fit of anger. She sat up very straight in the cedar chair where she was meditating, in the highest room in her tower, ripped apart her heavy dalmatic of yellow brocade, enriched with pearl lilies and foliage, broke the steel mirror that had just given her the odious news on the floor, and, full of towering rage, seized the enchanted toad that she used in her spell-casting by the hind leg, and threw it with all her might into the flames of the hearth, where it sizzled, crackled and hissed, and evaporated like a dry leaf.

Having done that, slightly calmer, she opened the panels of the high window, the leaden mesh of which enclosed dwarves blowing horns, and leaned out over the countryside. It was all white with snow, and, in the cold night air, slow scattered snowflakes, like cotton wool, extended all the way to the horizon a strange ermine, with inverted spots, white against a black background.

A great redness was illuminating the snow at the foot of the tower, and the Queen knew that it was the fire of the kitchens—the royal kitchens, where the cooking-pots were preparing the evening feast, for this was happening on the Sunday of Epiphany, and there was a great feast at the castle. And the wicked Queen Imogine could not help smiling in the blackness of her soul, because she knew that, at that very moment, a marvelous peacock was roasting for the mouth of the King, whose liver she had treacherously replaced with a salmagundi of lizard eggs and henbane, a horrible concoction that ought to complete the derangement of the old monarch's mind and banish forever from that unsteady consciousness the sweet memory of Princess Neigefleur.

Why had the frail and tender face of Neigefleur, with its big blue eyes and insipid doll-like features also undertaken to surpass her in beauty—her, the marvelous Imogine of the Golden Isles? Had it been necessary for her to come to this nasty little kingdom of Aquitaine only to hear cried aloud at every hour of the day, by the wind in the hedgerows and the roses in the flower-beds, and even by her mirror, a veridical mirror animated by the fays: "Your beauty is divine, and charms birds and humans alike, Queen Imogine, but Princess Neigefleur is more beautiful than you!" The little pest!

Then she had given her neither truce nor respite; there had been no villainy of which she had not accused the little Princess, like a true wicked stepmother, in order to depreciate her in the mind of the King; but the old imbecile, blinded by affection, had only listened with one ear, infatuated as he was with sensual passion for the beauty of his witch-queen.

Even poisons had had no purchase on that frail child's body; her innocence or the fays had protected her. The Queen still remembered, with rage, the day when, unable to bear it any longer, she had had the frightened little Princess undressed by her serving-women so that her quivering shoulders might be whipped until they bled; she had wanted to see that dazzling nudity finally tamed and spoiled by the rods; but the rods, in the hands of megaeras, had been changed into peacock feathers which had done nothing but flick and tickle the skin of the shivering virgin.

It was then, exasperated with spite, that she had resolved to kill her. She had strangled her with her royal hands and had her transported by night to the edge of the park, ready to accuse some troop of bohemians of the murder. Unexpected good fortune! She had not even had to make use of that fine invention with regard to the King; the wolves had taken charge of the affair; Princess Neigefleur had simply disappeared, and the proud stepmother had been triumphant, when her magic mirror, interrogated, had brought her sickeningly down to earth. She had avenged herself, to be sure, by getting rid of her for the moment, but she was not much further forward, since her rival was still alive, asleep under the protective guard of dwarves!

Very perplexed, she went to fetch from the depths of a cupboard the desiccated head of a hanged man, which she consulted on important occasions, and, having placed it on a large book open on a lectern, she lit three candles of green wax and plunged deep into sinister thought.

✳

Now she was walking, a long way—a very long way—from the sleeping palace, in the great silence of the frozen forest, the forest like an immense madrepore: she had thrown over her white silk robe a brown woolen cloak, which made her resemble some old sorcerer, and, her proud profile drawn back into the dark hood, she hastened past the feet of enormous oaks, whose snow-bleached trunks looked like great penitents themselves. Some of them, with their branches raised high in the shadows, seemed to be cursing her with all the strength of long fleshless arms; others, bent in strange attitudes, appeared to be kneeling on the edge of the path; one might have thought they were monks at prayer, with hoods of frost, all in bizarre procession, their hands singularly jointed and stiff above the snow, where muffled footfalls made no sound.

It was almost pleasant in the forest, the snow having rendered it torpid, and the Queen, entirely focused on her project, hastened her silent progress, the flaps of her cloak hermetically gathered over some sort of object, which was vaguely stirring and whimpering.

It was a six-month-old child, which she had stolen in passing from the bedroom of some serving-woman, and which she was carrying on this calm and mild winter night in order to cut its throat as midnight chimed, as was prescribed, at a crossroads. . . .

The elves, enemies of the gnomes, would all come running to drink the warm blood, and she would charm them with her crystal flute, a flute with three holes, reliable in magical incantations. Once charmed, the obedient elves would guide her through the maze of the paralyzed forest to the dwarves' grotto.

The entrance would be visible and gaping throughout the blessed night of the Epiphany, as on the night of Christmas. On those two nights, all enchantment is suspended by the omnipotent grace of Our Lord, and every cavern and subterranean hiding-place of the gnomes, guardians of buried treasures, is accessible to human feet. She would go into the lair, and, dispersing the frightened troop of kobolds with her emerald, would approach the glass coffin and force the lock, breaking the walls if necessary, and would strike her sleeping rival in the heart. This time, she would not escape.

But as she hastened, ruminating her vengeance, under the delicate white corals and arborescences of the frosty forest, psalms and voices suddenly rose up, a crystalline vibration ran through the numbed branches, the entire forest quivered like a harp, and the Queen, immobilized by amazement, saw a singular cortege advancing.

Under the cloudy winter sky, in the sparkling décor of a snowy clearing, there were dromedaries and fine thoroughbred horses, and palanquins of shiny multicolored silk, standards surmounted by crescents, golden orbs threaded on long iron-tipped lances, litters and turbans. Negro children, utterly diabolical in their green silk gandouras, were treading nervously through the snow, rings illuminated by gemstones tinkling at their ankles, and, but for the cheerful chatter of their laughter, one might have thought them little statues of black marble. They were hurrying in the footsteps of majestic patriarchs, diademed with soft fabrics striped with gold; the gravity of their haughty profiles continued in the silky foam of long white beards, and immense silk burnooses, the same silvery white as their beards, opened over heavy robes, nocturnal blue or auroral pink, florid with gemstones and golden arabesques; and the palanquins, in which veiled women could be vaguely glimpsed as if in a dream, oscillated on the backs of dromedaries; and the light of the moon, which had just risen, was reflected from the silk of the standards.

Penetrating perfumes and musks of cinnamon, benzoin and nard, were exhaled in blue swirls from incense-burners studded with brilliant enamels, between ebony black fingers, playing the role of cassolettes, and under the rising moon, the psalms burst firth, not so much sung as twittered in a soft Oriental language, as if unrolled in the gauze of veils and the fumes of the incense-burners.

The Queen, who had stopped behind a tree-trunk, had recognized the Mage Kings: the negro king Gaspar, the young sheik Melchior, and old Balthazar; they were going, as they had two thousand years before, to render their adoring homage to the divine Infant.

They had already passed by.

And the Queen, livid beneath her shepherd's cloak, remembered too late that on the night of Epiphany, the presence of the Magi marching toward Bethlehem breaks the power of evil spells, and that no sortilege is possible in the nocturnal air, which is as if impregnated with the myrrh of incense-burners.

She had therefore made a futile journey. The leagues she had traveled through the phantom forest became futile; her perilous expedition in the frost and snow would have to be recommenced.

She tried to take a step in a backward direction, but the child she was clutching under her cloak was strangely heavy in her arms; it had become as heavy as lead, and fixed her there, motionless in the snow—the snow that was accumulating around her strangely, through which her stiffened feet could no longer advance.

A horrible charm held her prisoner in the spectral forest; it was certain death if she could not break the circle. But where could she obtain help? All the evil spirits remain prudently in their retreats on the luminous night of Epiphany; only the good spirits, friends of the humble and the suffering, risk going abroad. The insidious Queen Imogine had the idea of appealing to the gnomes, to help her, the good lords clad in green and hooded with primroses who had collected Neigefleur. And, knowing them to be childishly fond of music, she had the strength to take her crystal flute from under her cloak and raise it to her lips.

She was weakening under the weight of the child, which had become akin to a block of ice; her feet, clutched by the blue-tinted snow, were turning black, and her violet lips only found soft and melancholy sounds, of a poignant sadness and a tender voluptuousness, the dolorous and captivating adieux of a soul in agony; resignedly, she still attempted, in vague hope, a futile appeal.

And while all the lies of her life commiserated on her lips, her eyes avidly searched the gloom of the clearing, the shadow of the trees, the tortuous furrows of the roots and the stumps left by woodcutters: the equivocal vegetal profiles in which gnomes initially manifest themselves.

Suddenly, the Queen shuddered. From all the points of the clearing, a multitude of glittering eyes were focused on her; it was like a circle of yellow stars closing in on her. They were between all the trees; they were in all the roots of the oaks; they were far away and close at hand; and every pair of eyes was fulgurant, phosphorescent, at half the height of a man, in the night.

It was the gnomes—finally! And the Queen stifled a cry of joy that almost immediately froze her with terror; she had just perceived two pointed ears above each pair of eyes, and below each pair of eyes, a furry muzzle and chops drawn back from white teeth.

Her magic flute had only summoned the wolves.

Her body was found the next day, torn apart by the beasts. Thus died, on a clear winter night, the wicked Queen Imogine.

GRIMALDINE
WITH THE GOLDEN HAIR

REGNIER GRIMALDI, Sire de Monaco, returning from conquering London for the King of France and regaining his estates in stages through the Duchy of Bourgogne and the realm of Provence, had stopped briefly in Avignon. Our Holy Father the Pope was then holding court there in great merriment, with reciters of sonnets, singers of ballads, mimes and mummers and other troubadours, and, among those so-called Compagnons du Gai Savoir, whose company is a sin for men of the Church, was a certain Galeas Alesti, a Florentine by origin and a poet by chance, who came to His Holiness' table that evening to celebrate, assisting himself with the mandolin, an incomparable Genoese beauty already famous throughout Provence and the Italian marches for her long, supple blonde hair, the most marvelous woman's fleece that had ever been seen on the Mediterranean coast since that of Mary Magdalen—who, as everyone knows, is the patron saint of Provence, and reposes in the Grotte de la Sainte-Baume, in the perfumed solitudes of the plain of Aups, half way up the flank of the Pilon.

Isabelle Asinari was the name of that beauty helmed with golden red hair, like that of Duc Achilleus himself, proclaimed the Florentine's verses:

And who bore on her milky breast
The August sun as pure invest . . .

as a couplet of a rondello by a Tourangean minstrel—a petty actor gone astray in Languedoc who had somehow ended up at the papal court—added by way of embroidery.

In brief, that Isabelle Asinari was making all the scrapers of strings and chasers of chimeras in the Palace of Avignon delirious. Her name and her eulogy were upon all lips, and the Sire de Monaco, a devotee of Mary Magdalen, like every good Provençal, making enquiries about that tonsorial rival of the sinner beloved by Our Lord, found himself smitten with a strange curiosity and perhaps a nascent amour, when he learned that Isabelle Asinari was a pious daughter, virtuous and living honestly in Genoa in the house of her father, a scrap metal dealer in the harbor district.

He desired to see this young woman who was as golden-haired as a Homeric hero, and, taking leave of His Holiness, he quit Avignon by night and went in great impatience to the port of Marseilles, chartered a ship there and, without even twitching the tiller toward his rock of Monaco, set a course for Genoa—already, poor fellow, in a raging amorous fever.

Grimaldi found the beauty in the paternal dwelling, sitting at her spinning-wheel. The house of the Genoese overlooked the harbor, and the little room where his daughter worked was illuminated by a window from which one could see the sea. Now, when the Sire de Monaco was introduced into that room, all the blue of the sky and all the blue of the sea were coming in through the little bay of the casement, open because of the heat; a large red lily, placed in a vase in the corner of the window, was quivering and trembling luminously in the breeze, and the daughter of the Genoese, her forehead pure and her face narrow, with long lowered eyelids, was sitting motionless beneath her red-gold hair, a creature of ivory, so mat was her complexion, against that intense azure in which the flower was ablaze. And Grimaldi found that the poets had not lied.

No, the Florentine had not lied, nor the rondello of the little Tourangean, nor any of the others. Delicate and pale, with her hair and her long lowered eyelashes, Isabelle Asinari was as beautiful as the statue of a saint framed in the blue of a stained-glass window, but her own stained-glass was all the azure of the Mediterranean. Thus aureoled, smiling, with her eyes closed, one might have thought that Isabelle was asleep, and Grimaldi, an anguish in his heart, was gazing at her silently, when the beauty slowly—very slowly—raised her eyelids; Grimaldi fell to his knees and saluted the young woman as a Moor might have saluted the dawn, with his forehead on the floor and his arms parted.

For Grimaldi, a dawn had indeed broken: the dawn of amour had risen. There was a moment of eternity . . . but, as Grimaldi was as devoted to the saints as he was fervently amorous of young women, he asked Isabelle's father for her hand, and as he was a very powerful lord of high lineage and insolently rich, he obtained permission to marry the beautiful tawny-haired spinner the very next day. She, pink from the temples to the base of the neck—although it could be divined that she was pink elsewhere too—had already allowed the impatient Regnier to take the tips of her pink fingers, which he covered with kisses.

There was a magnificent wedding, the splendor of which astonished the century; then, when the celebrations were over, Grimaldi took his wife to his rock of Monaco. Although they were accustomed to the most radiant sunlight, the dazzled Monegasques saluted the radiant advent of the blondest of princesses, and a saying ran around the land consecrating the beauty of the new bride: "It's now on Monaco that the sun of Genoa rises."

Then Regnier returned to the sea and his life as a corsair in the service of the Lily of France, and the blonde Asinari remained a trifle sad, looking out over the blue sea in the embalmed solitude of her rock, florid with cactus and haloed by towers.

No matter how much in love one was in those days, if one was in the King's service, the Lily came before love.

Now, during one of the brief truces when England and France recovered their breath, one evening when Monaco was in Paris, as a guest of the Queen, the courtiers, handsome sons and darlings of the bedchamber, Adonis-ed, lustrous and emitting delicate odors in their leotards of shiny silk, were mounting assaults of boasting and noisy vanity, all swollen with the pride of their successes, and obligingly detailing the miraculous and secret beauties of their lovers, each outbidding the last, all as vain as blackbirds, with their hands caressing their necklaces. Grimaldi sat to one side, listening, rather morosely, with his lips taut, to all that boasting.

"What about you, Grimaldi?" asked the Queen, addressing the somber individual. "You don't have any beauty about whom to boast, then? Valiant as you are, your heart must be devoid of love for you to sit there with that absent gaze and that stitched mouth. What! Don't you like the ladies, Monaco? That would be bad for a brave man like you."

To which Regnier shook his head disdainfully. "How can I respond to Your Majesty? In my country, the women have the sway of the waves in their hips, with all the sun in their smile, and the changing blue of the sea in their eyes. I'm from Provence, Madame."

And as all the peacocks and popinjays of courtiers sniggered at the amorous Monaco and all the women of his Provence, who would not have replied to them?

"The Princess of Monaco, Messeigneurs, is so beautiful that, in order to go in quest of her in Genoa, at the home of her father, an iron merchant, I chartered a ship in the port of Marseilles, even though I had never seen her, because her reputation had crossed the sea. The Princess of Monaco is famous on all the coasts of Provence and Italy, and, among other treasures and rarities, no woman in the world has ever possessed such long and supple blonde hair since Saint Mary Magdalen. That, at least, is what is said in my land of azure. I have responded, Messieurs!"

To which the Queen, slightly piqued, for she was not a little proud and she also had long and supple golden hair, said: "In truth, Monaco, you make me curious to see this famous and magnificent hair. Can we not bring that luminous fleece to court?"

Grimaldi stood up before the gracious Queen's throne. "Her Majesty's desires are orders. I shall, therefore, Madame, go and fetch the tresses that you desire to see." And with a deep bow, he quit the palace, escorted to the threshold by a sudden silence.

He was absent for two long months, and the courtiers, whom he had mortified, resumed their arrogance and their backbiting: "That Monaco surely commanded his princess with bewitching hair from some local sorceress." What masque was he about to bring them? "Some dark-skinned individual, no doubt—these Provençal women! Or some Mooress bought from pirates!"

The slanderous gossip followed its course, and the Queen began to lend an ear to the malicious words, for she was a woman, although a queen, cheerful and denigatory by nature. Then one beautiful August evening, the heralds suddenly announced Regnier Grimaldi.

The blonde Majesty got up from her throne. Monaco was alone.

"Alone! Monaco, are you toying with us?"

No, not alone, for two valets dressed in his livery were following Grimaldi, carrying a heavy iron box covered in crimson Venetian velvet.

They set the box down before the throne and, Monaco having opened it, he took out a long and heavy stream of shiny golden silk, smooth and fluid; a heavy skein of living gold, a sheet of light and perfumed amber, which one might have thought woven from the freshness of dawn, and the entire gloomy palace was illuminated by it.

Monaco, standing, combed the fleece of light with his fingertips.

The Queen had understood. "I asked for the Princess, Monaco, not her hair. How have you been able to commit this sacrilege, this murder, this crime against beauty? What! You have shaven your wife's hair!"

Then Grimaldi said: "Her Majesty demanded that I bring her the hair, not the Princess. First of all, the woman is for me alone; I keep her. You desired to see the hair; is not my tender Queen's wish granted?"

And as the dazzled Queen, her hand joined in ecstasy and her eyes wide, never ceased repeating: "But to shave such hair is a sacrilege, a murder, a crime against beauty," the terrible man added:

"Let Her Majesty be reassured that I only cut one lock of it."

A PARTIAL LIST OF SNUGGLY BOOKS